Firebird Feathers

Judy Lunsford

Firebird Feathers

a short story

Judy Lunsford

Copyright Information

Firebird Feathers

For Kate

Once upon a time there were three witches. They were sisters and they each lived alone in their own hut deep in the darkest forest.

The oldest sister was feared by all the surrounding villages. She was known as mean and wicked and most people left her alone. Occasionally, a knight would show up, intending to kill her. But he stood no chance against her in her own home. She had a collection of human skulls on her fence posts surrounding her hut to warn away any other brave young men that came to try to challenge her.

The middle sister was also known by the surrounding villages. But she was loved and trusted by those who came to her in need. The middle sister was often willing to give aid to the sick and injured. She also offered potions and lucky charms to those who could convince her that they were in need.

The oldest sister and the middle sister did not get along at all, for they had very differing views about how a witch should behave amongst the human world.

The oldest thought witches were better and more important than others because of their power given to them by mother earth.

The middle sister felt that witches were given the power to aid humans and other creatures and that they were to behave with benevolence and authority over the poor wretched villagers that were tasked to them.

The youngest of the three sisters had a secret. She lived deep in the dark woods and she wasn't known by the people of the villages. She wasn't mean, she didn't have to go up against young knights who were looking to prove themselves. She wasn't known for her healing or her spells and wasn't sought after by the sick of body, mind, or heart. But she did have her secret.

On All Hallows' Eve, the three sisters were in the forest collecting mushrooms for use in meals and potions. And in hopes of coming upon a firebird.

Firebirds were magical creatures that were exceedingly rare indeed. Coming across a firebird was considered to be very lucky and one who could even touch it was considered to have the most powerful magic themselves. A firebird could only be found on All Hallows' Eve, as it was the only day of the year that they could be seen with human eyes.

The youngest of the three sisters was the first to see the firebird. He was beautiful and regal, sitting tall in the tree with his red feathers blazing hot in the dappled sunlight that found him through the orange and yellow autumn leaves above. She could see waves of heat rippling off his body and into the air. His long tail dangled far below the branch he sat on and the plume on his head bobbled back and forth as he cocked his head to the side to look at her.

She ran over to her older sisters to point him out to them. She was so happy that she was the one that was lucky enough to see the bird first as he stared down at them.

The bird sat high up in a tree and looked down at them with a casual glance. He seemed unconcerned that the three witches below him were very excited to see him. For he was not at all excited to see them. He did, however, seem to have an interest in the youngest witch.

He shifted from one foot to the other on his perch and watched them with curiosity as they moved closer to him.

The three sisters whispered among themselves. The oldest sister wanted to capture the bird and kill him to drain his magical essence.

The middle sister wanted to catch him and bring him home as a pet, so she could utilize his magic when necessary.

The youngest sister wished she hadn't pointed the poor creature out to her sisters at all and looked up at the bird with apologetic eyes as her sister witches put together a plan.

The oldest witch had some leftover bread in her pocket. She had brought it with her in case she got hungry. She volunteered to use the bread to lure the bird out of his tree and down to the ground so they could capture the creature.

The middle sister had brought a large dark green cloak with her, in case she got cold deep in the forest. She said she could use the cloak to throw over the bird when he came down to the ground to eat the bread.

The two sisters agreed that they would decide what to do with the bird once he was captured.

The youngest sister watched the bird closely and hoped that he didn't like bread and that the crumbs that her oldest sister sprinkled on the ground would be of no interest to the bird.

The two older sisters put their plan into action, and much to the youngest sister's disappointment, the bird came down out of the tree and floated gracefully to the ground and started to eat the bits of bread that the oldest sister had scattered on the ground.

The middle sister threw her cloak over the bird and it squawked in anger as it thrashed around under the heavy green cloak.

The three sisters jumped towards the bird, with the older two sisters trying to grab the bird as he thrashed around under the cloak.

The youngest sister, feeling for the bird, lunged forward and grabbed the corner of the cloak. She pretended to stumble backwards and pulled the cloak hard, releasing the bird from her sisters' attempts to capture him.

The bird's head appeared out the far end of the cloak from where the youngest sister still held on to it, and as the bird spread his wings, he knocked over the older two sisters through the cloak and forced them to stumble backwards.

All three sisters scrambled on the ground to try to regain their footing, but it was too late. The firebird took off in a burst of flames that forced the older two sisters to cover their faces in order to protect themselves from the power of the bird.

He soared high into the air and off into the evening sunset.

The youngest sister looked at her hand and found that he had accidentally pulled two tail feathers from the bird when she tried to rescue him. She hid the feathers in her skirt pocket quickly, before her sisters could see.

She handed her middle sister back her cloak and stared at the ground.

The middle sister snatched the cloak away from the youngest sister and the oldest sister swore curses at the youngest for her clumsiness and stupidity, and for costing them the chance at obtaining a firebird for another year.

The three sisters went back to their homes, the older two in anger and disappointment. The youngest went home in relief and was glad that the firebird had gotten away safely.

Late that night, under the light of the full moon, there was a knock at the youngest sister's door.

She climbed out of bed and looked out the window to see a tall man dressed as a knight standing at her front door.

She went to her door and opened it just slightly.

"Hello?" she said. She felt like her voice was stuck in her throat.

"I am here on behalf of Magnus the Magnificent," the knight said. "He has sent me to bring you back to the royal castle. You were chosen to be his apprentice, should you accept this honor."

"I'm sorry," the youngest sister opened the door wider. "You must be looking for one of my sisters."

"No," the knight shook his head. "I was sent by Magnus himself and his directions to your humble home were very specific."

"You must really have the wrong sister," she said again. "For you see, I have no magical powers like my sisters do."

"And that is the secret that you have been hiding for all these years," a voice said from behind the knight.

The youngest sister squinted into the pale light that the moon cast down on the man that was standing behind the knight.

"Yes," she nodded. "It is."

The knight moved aside to let the other man pass.

He was an old man with a long white beard and a full head of white hair. He had bushy white eyebrows and he wore a long red cloak that seemed to flicker like firelight in the light of the full moon.

"You're Magnus?" the youngest sister said. "The warlock who serves the king?"

"Yes, I am," the old man said. "And what is your name?"

"My name is Nix," she said.

"You obtained something today, Nix," the old man said. "Did you not?"

The youngest sister nodded.

"May I see them?" Magnus asked.

Nix went inside and retrieved the two firebird feathers from the pocket of her skirt that was laying on a chair by the fire.

"Firebird feathers," Magnus nodded. "You do know that only one with the most powerful magic can touch a firebird."

"I didn't really touch him," Nyx said. "I was just trying to rescue him from my sisters."

"Yes," the old man nodded. "And I appreciate that greatly."

"You're-" Nix started.

"Yes," Magnus said. "I was that firebird. And the fact that you hold two of my feathers in your hand proves that you touched me while we were out in the forest today."

"But I have no magical powers," Nyx said. "Not like my sisters."

"That is where you are wrong," Magnus said. "You have more magic than both of your sisters combined, you just need to learn how to use it. And I have chosen you to become my apprentice because of your vast powers and your mercy."

Nyx looked at the two feathers in her hand.

Magnus smiled at the young girl and said, "Come with me and I will show you the power you have. I will train you to become the most powerful witch in the land. Be my apprentice and you can take my place as advisor to the king and become the head sorceress of the kingdom."

"Are you sure I have magic?" Nyx asked.

Magnus nodded. "I will teach you how to release the magic that is inside of you. You will become greater than your sisters, and they will no longer drain you of your power."

Nyx looked up at him in shock.

"Yes," he nodded. "Your secret isn't that you have no magic, it is that your sisters use you for your power."

"And I can escape them if I go with you?" she asked.

"Yes," Magnus said.

"But my middle sister, she does good with the magic," Nyx said. "She heals people."

"With stolen magic," Magnus said. "The people can come to you instead."

"What will happen to my sisters?" Nyx asked.

"Whatever you decide for their fate," Magnus said. "They have both committed a great crime in draining you of your power. Stealing magic from another is punishable by death."

Nyx stared at the feathers in her hands.

"Can I have them spared?" Nyx asked. "For they are my sisters."

"Only if you come with me," Magnus said. "Only if you work for the king can you have the authority to ask that your sisters be spared."

Nyx looked at the feathers in her hands.

"So, you were the firebird?" she asked.

"Yes," Magnus nodded. "The most powerful magical creature in existence. And you will be the next firebird, with my training."

Nyx ran her fingers along the soft, hot barbs of the feathers.

"We must hurry. It is almost midnight, and the apprentice ceremony can only be done in the moonlight on All Hallows' Eve," Magnus said.

She smiled up at Magnus and said, "I accept your offer."

More books by Judy Lunsford:

Gamers
Schemers

Fire Lily
Bezbell
Kirog

Moonlight Magic
Moonlight Melody

The Red Dart
Shadow Mountain

The Portal Wars
The Grimoires

For YA:

Life Unscripted
The Secret Gondal Society

Short Stories:
The Dark of Night
Fairy Short Stories
Fairy Tales & Nightmares
Fantasy Faire
First Stories
Magic from the Dark
Story Hoard
The Wild Hunt

Thank you for reading.
If you enjoyed this book, you can find more stories at
JudyLunsford.com
or your favorite online retailer.